SBN 361 05285 5
Copyright © 1980 Walt Disney Productions
Published September 1981 by Purnell Books, Berkshire
House, Queen Street, Maidenhead, Berkshire
Made and printed in Great Britain by Purnell and Sons
Limited, Paulton (Bristol) and London

StMichael

WALT DISNEY PRODUCTIONS'

the Fox and the Hound

The Baby Fox is Found

On a misty morning in spring, a mother fox was running for dear life through the woodland, followed by a hunter and his hound. The fox would have run even faster, but she was carrying something in her mouth, something soft and small and precious. It was her baby cub. The hound was barking loudly as he knew he was catching up with the fox.

The mother fox was chased into some open farmland and she ran beside a fence, seeking cover. Here the grass and weeds grew tall and, still running, she dropped her little one into a thick patch of grass and made for a wooded slope. The hunter and his hound could see her clearly and two shots rang out, but the fox disappeared over the horizon, running faster now that she had nothing to carry.

As the two shots rang out, crack! crack! the peace of the morning was shattered. A flock of birds rose from the trees and made off with warning cries, and many small, furry creatures crouched further into their holes or burrows.

But one bird did not fly away. She was an owl called Big Mama, and her round, staring eyes missed nothing that went on within sight of the tree where she lived. She had watched the chase, and had seen the fox drop something into the long grass by the fence. She cruised slowly off with steady beats of her strong wings, and landed on the post of the fence. She looked down and saw the little cub, trembling and alone,

peeping out between the grasses. He was quite unlike her own children, her little owlets, who were covered with feathers and had claws and curved beaks, but her heart went out to him. She wanted to warm him and comfort him.

But Big Mama was a very wise bird. She knew she could not be a mother to the cub. She would need help, and the only person she could think of was Widow Tweed who lived on a farm close by. She could not immediately decide how to get the cub and Widow Tweed together, so she went to look for two friends of hers whom she knew would help if they could. One friend was a woodpecker called Boomer, and the other a sparrow called Dinky.

She left the little cub, assuring him that she would soon be

back, and flew to a nearby tree, where she could hear the tap-tap-tapping of Boomer's beak on the bark. Dinky was perched on a branch above, watching.

"Boomer!" shouted Big Mama, "I've something to tell you." But Boomer took no notice. He was too busy watching the hole he had made in the trunk and so was Dinky.

"I'm sure that caterpillar Squeeks is hiding in there," Boomer whispered. "We'll get him this time."

"We will, for certain," whispered Dinky. "Peck a bit harder."

The tapping went on until Big Mama shouted again, still louder. "I need you two, I need you badly, come with me."

Both birds grumbled, but they went with Big Mama to the fence, perched on it and looked down, straight at the little cub, who had parted the grass and was looking up at them.

"Oh, the poor little fellow!" said Boomer.

"He's only a baby," said Dinky.

"We're going to find someone to look after him," said Big Mama. "Widow Tweed would do, but how do we get him there?" There was a silence while they all thought. Then Dinky had an idea and whispered it to the others in an excited voice. They agreed and all flew towards the Widow's farmhouse, where Boomer rapped smartly on the door with his beak. Presently the Widow opened the door wide.

"I thought I heard someone knocking," she said, and then looked towards the clothes-line where her washing was hung out to dry. There, to her horror, she saw Big Mama and Dinky tugging at her bloomers. As she looked, they pulled them off the line and flew away with them in their beaks.

"Oh, those pesky birds," screamed Widow Tweed. "Come back here at once," she cried. But the birds went on and dropped the bloomers so that they fell on top of the little cub,

covering him completely. When the Widow, much out of breath, reached the spot and picked up her washing, she saw what was underneath.

"Why, bless my soul, it's a baby fox."

She gathered him in her arms and stroked him and hushed him, talking softly and lovingly. She carried him back to the farm and soon he lay quietly in her lap, sucking a bottle of milk like a human baby. She called him Tod.

The three birds—Big Mama, Boomer and Dinky—sat on the window sill and watched what was going on inside. They were proud and happy that their plan had worked so well. They heard the Widow say, "I'm not going to be lonely anymore."

Half a mile away, outside a cabin, a large hound lay sleeping in the barrel which was his home. His name was Chief and his master was a hunter, the very hunter who had chased Tod's mother.

Chief, who slept lightly, heard the distant sound of his master's truck approaching, and was wide awake in a second. As the old truck rattled to a stop outside, Chief watched the Hunter rummaging in the back and saw him lift up a sack. He held it out in front of Chief.

"I've got a surprise for you," said the Hunter.

Chief strained on his lead, and sniffed the sack suspiciously. He thought he saw something inside the sack stir a little.

"Now take it easy," said his master, putting his hand deep into the sack and bringing out a small puppy. "How's this for a huntin' dog, Chief? His name is Copper."

Copper was bright brown like his name. When he felt the ground under his feet he walked unsteadily towards Chief, sat up and reached towards the big dog's face and licked his nose with a warm, pink tongue.

"He's just a little pup, now," said the Hunter, "but he'll grow."

Chief jerked his head back and looked displeased, while little Copper wiggled his tail with excitement, wanting to make friends.

"Copper is for you to look after," went on the Hunter. "You must train him to be a really good huntin' dog. He's got a lot

to learn, and you are the one to teach him. No one else can do it.''

Chief rather liked this idea, but he was not sure that he wanted this small, demanding little creature spoiling his peaceful life. He turned round and retreated into his barrel, not noticing that little Copper had slipped in beside him. Chief growled, and pushed him out with his great paw. Copper came back at once, still wiggling his tail and smiling up at him.

There was a pause, then Copper tried again and was not pushed out. He snuggled down beside Chief and laid his head trustfully on Chief's leg. Soon they were both asleep.

Tod and Copper become Friends

While little Copper grew bigger and wiser, little Tod the fox cub flourished under the Widow's loving care. At first he learned to explore the farmhouse, then the yard, then the land around. Of course, his new freedom gave him many chances to get into mischief. Once, when the Widow was milking Abigail the cow, Abigail's swishing tail hit Tod and knocked him over.

"Don't go so close, Tod," said the Widow, "and you,

Abigail, remember that Tod is part of the family and be patient with him."

There was a hen and her three chicks in the barn. Tod meant no harm, but the mother hen was afraid and she squawked loudly when she saw him. Abigail mooed and the bell she wore round her neck swung and hit the hen, who squawked louder than ever. This upset the Widow—who fell off her milking stool, just as Abigail's swishing tail knocked her glasses off her nose. The angry hen chased Tod out of the barn and Abigail's foot kicked over the pail of milk. There was milk and muddle everywhere.

The Widow picked Tod up by the scruff of his neck and began to scold him. Tod, looking guilty, licked her ear as a sign that he was sorry.

"You little imp," she said. "Now run off and play and stay out of mischief!"

Tod ran off and soon saw Boomer and Dinky, in a tree as usual, chasing the caterpillar Squeeks, whom they were determined to catch and eat. They thought he had gone down a hole in the hollow tree, where he had hidden before.

"Quiet!" whispered Dinky, "I can hear him moving about. You peck here, Boomer."

Boomer pecked furiously at the hole, and brought out a piece of bark. Though he didn't know it, Squeeks was clinging to the other side of the bark.

"There's nothing in that hole. It's empty," Boomer sighed. Then Dinky caught a glimpse of the caterpillar.

"Catch him, Boomer. Trap him!" he shouted, but once more Squeeks was too clever for them. He vanished down another hole.

"You've lost us our breakfast!" Dinky complained.

"I've bent my beak pecking so hard," said Boomer.

Tod saw that the birds were not going to play with him, as

he had hoped, so he ran off, chasing a butterfly.

"What a fuss about catching a worm for breakfast," he thought to himself.

While Tod was growing up and getting into mischief, Copper was growing up, too, in the Hunter's cabin. One day, the two dogs were drinking from the same bowl, when Copper lifted his head and sniffed.

"I can smell something new," he said. Chief lifted his great head and sniffed too.

"Don't you know the smell of master cooking his bacon?" he said scornfully. But Copper was not satisfied.

"It's a smell I've never met before," he repeated, "and I'm

going to find out exactly what it is."

"Master will be angry if you wander away by yourself," said Chief. But Copper had made up his mind. He ran off.

The strange scent was the smell of fox, and led Copper to a hollow log where Tod was playing. Tod was peering through a hole in the log when he met Copper's nose, coming through from the other side, sniffing busily.

"What are you smelling?" asked Tod.

"I'm on the trail of something, I don't know what," Copper replied. Then their noses met and Copper cried out: "Why, it's you! It's you I've been trailing."

"I'm a fox called Tod. What's your name?"

"Mine's Copper and I'm a hound dog. Shall we play hide-and-seek?"

Tod agreed and they had a wonderful game, over and under

the log, in and out of the bushes. Big Mama the owl watched and marvelled that the fox and hound should play together, as they are natural enemies. But the two got on so well that her fears died down. Then the Hunter whistled from the hill.

"I must go," said Copper and ran off to the cabin to be greeted by a scowling master who pointed sternly to his barrel. Copper went obediently inside and sat down sadly. The fun was over.

Tod had taken a fancy to his new companion, and early the next morning he sneaked over to the cabin and called softly, "Copper! Copper!"

Copper peeped out of his barrel and made sure that Chief was asleep and snoring. Then he crept out like a shadow and joined Tod by the fence. They tumbled and rolled together before running off to the water-hole to swim.

While they played, Big Mama sang a song from her tree. Sometimes they listened and sometimes they didn't, but both remembered some of the words afterwards:

When you're the best of friends,
Having so much fun together,
You're not even aware
You're such a funny pair.
You're the best of friends,
Life's a happy game:
You could clown around for ever.
Neither one of you sees
Your boundaries.

Life's one happy game,
If only the world wouldn't get in the way:
If only people would let you play.
They say you're both being fools:
You're breaking all the rules.
They can't understand
The magic of your wonderland
When you're the best of friends.
When these wonderful moments have passed,
Will that friendship last?
Who can say?

"Copper, you're my very best friend," said Tod.

"And you're mine, too," said Copper.

"We'll always be friends for ever and ever, won't we?"

"Yes, for ever and ever."

It was fun in the water-hole, diving and splashing, until the Hunter and Chief appeared in the distance. The Hunter was very angry.

"We've got to teach that Copper pup not to stray away from the cabin," growled the Hunter. "If he's going to make a good huntin' dog he'll have to learn to do what he's told."

The Hunter whistled and Copper heard him, then the Hunter whistled a second time. Copper climbed sadly up the bank and shook himself.

"I've got to go home, Tod. He does sound cross."

"I'll see you tomorrow," said Tod. "Don't forget."

"No, I won't."

When Tod next visited the cabin he found Copper very miserable, tied up tightly so that he couldn't leave his barrel.

"Master says I must stay at home, so he's tied me up."

Chief was snoring in his barrel and Tod went nearer to have a good look at the sleeping monster.

"Gosh, he's ever so big! But his ears aren't as big as yours, Copper. Just look at those teeth!"

"You be careful of them," warned Copper.

Tod went even nearer and almost touched Chief's nose.

Chief opened one eye and saw Tod in front of him and knew him to be a fox.

"It's a FOX!" exclaimed Chief, pushing Tod to the back of his barrel and pinning him there firmly.

"Run, Tod, run for your life," shouted Copper. "He'll get you."

Tod managed to squeeze past the enraged Chief and make for the chicken house. Chief, angrier than ever, tried to follow,

but he was tied to his barrel and only by using all his strength did he manage to drag the heavy barrel loose and pull it after him.

This commotion upset the chickens who flew about wildly, squawking and fluttering. All this noise, plus the barking of Chief, woke the Hunter who snatched up his gun and dashed out of the cabin, pulling up his trousers with one hand. He saw the fox among the frightened chickens and fired hastily, but Tod skidded to a standstill, and doubled back. The shot missed and Tod streaked for home and safety along a narrow country road, followed by the noise of more shots.

The Hunter saw that he would never catch the fox on foot, so he went back and jumped into his old, rattling truck. Tod had a good start and when he saw the Widow ahead, taking her milk cans to market in her Model T Ford, he decided to try to overtake her and ask for help.

He leapt on to the top of a stone wall and tore along it, and as he drew level with the car he gave a mighty jump, right through the car window, and into the back.

The Hunter's last shot hit the wall and the pellets bounced off. He braked behind the Widow's car and aimed at her milk cans. These he hit easily and made several holes through which the milk gushed out.

The Widow stopped, jumped out and pulled the shotgun out of the Hunter's hands. He was too surprised to prevent her.

"Watch it!" he shouted. "That gun's loaded."

The Widow pressed the trigger and emptied the gun into his radiator. Steam boiled up and water spurted out.

"It isn't loaded now," she cried angrily, and handed the gun back to its owner.

The two had a violent argument in the narrow road, the Hunter saying that Tod was a thieving fox who had been after his chickens, trying to kill them. The Widow replied that she knew Tod inside and out. He would never harm a living creature, chicken or anything else.

"If ever I find that thieving fox on my property again, I'll blast him to bits," yelled back the Hunter.

He drove off, his truck rattling even more than usual.

Summer is Over

The next day, the Widow tried to keep Tod in the farm-house with her, for safety, but he was restless and unhappy. By standing on his hind legs he could just see out of the window and catch a glimpse of the cabin with the two barrels outside and the Hunter's old truck.

"Poor little chap," said the Widow, stirring something on the stove. "It's a real shame I have to keep you cooped up like this. But you know you did cause a lot of trouble yesterday."

She turned and looked out of the window with Tod, holding the curtain back so that she could get a better view of the

cabin. The Hunter was very busy, packing the back of his truck with all kinds of gear.

"Looks like the Hunter is going on a hunting trip—and a pretty long one, too. Well, good riddance."

She went back to her cooking, leaving Tod keeping watch by himself. He heard his friend Copper howling in the distance, and quietly climbed over the sill and dropped to the ground. Then he set off steadily towards the cabin. As he got nearer he saw that the Hunter was having trouble with his old truck. It refused to start, even when he gave it a kick.

At last the engine started up and the dogs barked with excitement. Copper was jumping up and down, and the Hunter bent down and patted his head.

"Well, Copper," he said, "me and Old Chief are going to teach you all about huntin', and it's about time, too."

He untied Copper's rope and Copper ran round in circles, even squeezing between his master's legs, waggling his tail non-stop. Chief was sitting proudly in the front seat, so Copper sprang on to the running board and on to the seat beside Chief, but he soon discovered that this was a mistake.

"Get into the back," said Chief gruffly, "you half-pint pup, you have to *earn* your right to sit up front with me."

Copper was puzzled, but he knew that Chief had to be obeyed and so he scrambled over the back of the seat, and landed among a mass of strange objects, most of them new to him. There were steel traps, nets and guns, and camping equipment. There were cooking pots, sleeping bags, blankets, knives, plates and mugs. There was everything a man and two dogs might want on a long hunting trip, living rough in all weathers.

As the truck moved off, Tod arrived on the scene, and Copper caught a glimpse of him. He howled as he saw his friend standing all by himself near the cabin. The two were very sad to be parted—they did not know for how long—as the truck disappeared in a cloud of dust.

As Tod sat miserably down, with his eyes fixed on the distant cloud of dust, Big Mama flew into sight and perched on Copper's empty barrel.

"Hey there, honey, what are you doing here?" she called.

"I just came over to say goodbye to my friend Copper," said Tod, "but I'm too late. He's gone away."

"But what would you have done if you'd come across that old Chief? He's no friend of young foxes like you."

"Oh, that silly old dog? I'm his match any day."

"Now be quiet a minute, Tod, and listen to me." Big Mama spoke so seriously that Tod lifted his head and gazed at her feathery face with its round, glowing eyes and curved beak.

Big Mama went on in the same, serious voice.

"Didn't you learn anything from what happened yesterday? You've got to learn and act accordingly, or it will be the end of you. Chief is a hunting dog who hunts foxes, and he'll hunt you and kill you. Or the Hunter will get you and hang you up from a nail on the wall. And your friend Copper is being trained to hunt, too. He'll be after you."

"Oh, Big Mama—I know Copper would never track me down. He's my best friend."

"Ha! Ha!" mocked Big Mama. "Your best friend now, perhaps, but Copper has gone away for a long time to learn to be a proper hunting dog. He'll have to learn to do exactly what he's told. If he's told to chase a little fox and get him out of his fox-hole, he'll do it. He'll have to. You must believe it."

Tod looked alarmed. "You mean that Copper, my best friend, will be my enemy?"

"Yes, I do."

"My *enemy*!" repeated Tod. "My *enemy*!"

Boomer and Dinky, the woodpecker and the sparrow, were listening to this conversation, perching on the roof of the barn.

"Come with us, Tod," said Dinky. "Just step over here into the barn and have a look. There's something you ought to see."

The two birds opened the barn door, which creaked on its hinges, and Tod went inside with them. What he saw filled him with fear and horror.

There, nailed on the barn wall, were the skins of many furry animals. There were rabbits and squirrels and rats, and others which Tod did not recognise.

"Why, that's awful. That's terrible," said Tod. "Those poor, poor things."

He looked so upset that Big Mama flew to his side and folded her warm, feathery wings round him, trying to comfort him.

"I'm sorry, Tod, honey," she whispered. "Copper's going to come back a trained hunting dog. A real killer."

"No! No!" wailed Tod. "Not my friend Copper. He won't ever change."

"I hope you're right, Tod."

"And we'll keep on being friends for ever, won't we, Big Mama?"

"Darling, forever is a long, long time and things have a way of changing," replied Big Mama, quietly.

Time Changes Things

The autumn came, with golden leaves dropping from the trees and drifting with the wind into the dogs' empty barrels. Then followed winter, with frost on the bare branches and icicles hanging from the fence and the roof. Snow fell lightly, first a few feathery flakes, then thicker and faster, making piles on the frozen ground. Little Squeeks the caterpillar poked his head out of the hole in the tree where he had been hiding. He looked around at the snowy world, shivering as an icy gust of wind reached him.

But in that second Squeeks had caught a glimpse of something cheerful and comforting. He saw the window of the Widow's farmhouse, lit by the leaping flames of the fire inside. He came right out of his hole and started to creep over the snow, heading towards the light and warmth.

There was a scarecrow beyond the fence, a wind-blown, tattered thing, and huddled together in its hat were Boomer and Dinky, both shivering.

"I really am cold," said Dinky.

"I'm freezing," agreed Boomer.

Then Dinky's sharp eyes spotted something moving over the snow.

"Hey, Boomer, there's that fuzzy worm down there. Let's go and get him."

Just then Squeeks looked back over his shoulder and saw his pursuers. He was approaching the farmhouse and he did the only thing possible—he dived into a bank of snow. Boomer and Dinky dived after him, and with Boomer's greater weight the snow bank collapsed, burying Dinky completely.

Boomer shook the snow off himself and thought he saw Squeeks moving, like a dark thread. He pecked fiercely with his strong beak and brought out Dinky.

"I've g-g-got him!" shouted Boomer excitedly, waving the angry Dinky.

"Do I look like a WORM!" raged Dinky.

"No, but I thought . . ."

"Then you were wrong. Wrong and stupid."

While the two were arguing, Squeeks crawled up the door towards the keyhole and disappeared through it.

"He's gone through the keyhole, Boomer," said Dinky, "I'm going to see what he's up to." He put his bright little eye to the hole and saw Squeeks clinging to the edge of a flower pot,

warming himself by the kitchen stove.

"He's warm and cosy by the fire, while we're freezing out here."

"Let me have a look," said Boomer, pushing Dinky aside and spying through the keyhole himself. He saw Squeeks climb off the flower pot and settle down in a basket of the Widow's knitting.

"Snug as a bug in a rug," exclaimed Boomer. "How do you like that?"

"We can't stay here shivering all the winter till our beaks are frozen," went on Boomer. "We must fly south to a warmer land and come back here in the spring. Then we can catch that caterpillar."

Big Mama peeped out as they flew by her tree, so they stopped to say goodbye.

"Cheerio, Big Mama. We're heading south."

"Goodbye, boys—see you next spring!"

While Tod was staring unhappily through the window of the farmhouse, eyes fixed on the empty barrels, Copper, many miles further north, was learning the skills of a trained hunting dog. At first he copied Chief in whatever he did. If Chief sniffed at a twig—then he sniffed. If Chief howled—then he howled. If Chief followed a scent, creeping along through the snow, then he went after him.

After some time, Copper found he need not always follow
the older dog, doing all he did. He could find a scent by
himself and set out on his own in pursuit. Soon he and Chief
were hunting separately, and it was more often Copper who
chased some game birds out of a tree so that the Hunter could
get a shot and bring one down.

Once the Hunter fired a successful shot and killed a bird Copper had hunted out for him, and when Chief came panting on the scene he saw his master patting Copper's shining head and heard him say, "Well done, little fellow, well done."

The Hunter was satisfied with his winter's hunting and began to pack up to go home. All the sleeping bags and traps and equipment were stowed in the back of the truck, with a pile of valuable skins.

When Chief climbed on to the running board, ready to jump into his old place in the front seat, he discovered Copper already sitting there, looking very pleased with himself. The old hound gave a low growl of disappointment and moved into the back. So the truck set off down the mountain side, bumping and rattling on its way north, with Copper sitting up in front and Chief at the back, among the baggage.

Spring had come to the countryside around the farmhouse and the cabin, and Dinky and Boomer flew back to their old homes. Big Mama was spring-cleaning her hole in the hollow tree. Grass was growing green in the meadows and early flowers were blooming. Tod came from under a pile of leaves where he had been dozing, and shook himself.

Big Mama picked a few leaves off Tod's head, not recognising him at first.

"Well, my goodness, who's here? Tod, honey, it's you!"

Dinky and Boomer flew down to land on a fence post. "Hello, Big Mama, we're back. We flew all the way," boasted Dinky.

"Yes we did, all the way from the south."

Big Mama was glad to see them. "It's been kind of quiet here without you boys around."

"Hello, there!" called Tod, wanting to join in.

Dinky and Boomer pretended they did not know who Tod was; he had grown so much, and changed.

"You can't be that skinny little cub we found by the fence post, in the long grass!" laughed Dinky.

Boomer rubbed his eyes with amazement and declared, "I just can't believe it's true."

"It's me all right," said Tod, "there's no doubt of that."

"He's got himself a real, fancy collar."

"And just look at his beautiful, bushy tail!"

Dinky and Boomer teased him and admired him, and Tod glowed with pleasure.

"Stop it, you two. I've been teased enough for one day," he said, smiling at them.

Just then they heard the farmhouse door creak and out came the Widow, carrying a very sickly-looking pot-plant in her hand. She had no idea that Squeeks the caterpillar was hidden in the plant.

"I don't understand—it was so healthy once," she said, "perhaps it's got too dry."

Getting nearer the cabin, the Hunter was looking forward to unpacking his gear and his collection of animal skins. Chief remained sulky and cross, growling if anyone touched him. The Hunter wanted his trusty old hound to be cheerful again.

"Come on, Chief," he said kindly; "just because you're not sittin' up front, that's no reason to pout. Why, if it weren't for you, Copper would never have turned out a good huntin' dog."

The Hunter turned and reached over to pat Chief and comfort him, but Chief only gave his master a disagreeable look.

"Yes, sir, now I got me the *best two dogs* there are in the world. The very best two dogs. Haven't I, Copper?"

Copper gave a howl which meant that he agreed.

Chief, still in a bad temper, put his two great paws over his ears to try to shut out the sound. The Hunter attempted to imitate Copper's howl, for fun, and as the truck stopped in front of the cabin a loud, wailing sound came from inside.

Tod had seen the truck in the distance and was running up the hill like mad, to see if he could catch it up. Big Mama was flying with him, above his head. The truck drove past.

"Look, Big Mama," said Tod, "Copper is back. Hasn't he grown big! Did you see him sitting up in the front?"

"Yes, I did, Tod. And did you see Chief at the back, sitting on a great big pile of skins? They were the skins of animals

that your friend Copper helped to track down.''

''I know, Big Mama. He's a proper hunting dog now.''

''You're right, Tod. He's a proper trained hunting dog and you are a fox. Don't you ever forget that.''

''All the same,'' said Tod, ''I've just got to find out if Copper is still my friend.''

''Well, honey,'' warned Big Mama, ''don't set your hopes too high. And take care.''

''Now don't you worry, Big Mama. I'll be very, very, careful. I won't go over to the cabin till tonight, when the Hunter and Chief are fast asleep.''

Outside the cabin, Copper was drinking water from his bowl. Then he had a good scratch and said to Chief, who was still in his barrel, ''Well, Chief, isn't it good to be home?''

''Huh!'' growled Chief, grumpily.

''Oh, come on, Chief,'' said Copper, wagging his tail. ''You aren't still cross, are you? Cheer up, do. Let's have a scuffle. Let's play as we used to.''

Chief came out of his barrel and the two dogs played together, chasing each other and wrestling. Copper got hold of

Chief's floppy ear and refused to let go.

"Oh, don't be silly, Copper, you over-grown pup. Let go!"

Chief's good nature turned to irritation in a moment, as he managed to pull his ear free. "You know, that was your trouble when you were away hunting," said Chief in a scolding voice.

"Come off it, old timer," protested Copper. "You still treat me like a pup. Why is that? I did some fine hunting, tracking down that vermin for you."

"Smellin' and trackin' aren't enough," Chief hadn't finished his lecture. "You've got to *think* nasty, too."

"Yes, yes, I know," Copper sighed. "I know only too well."

When darkness fell, Tod slipped from the farmhouse without the Widow knowing, and made off for the cabin. Both the Hunter's dogs were sleeping in their barrels. Tod moved cautiously towards Copper's barrel and whispered, "Copper! Hey there, Copper! It's me. It's your friend Tod."

"I thought it was you, Tod. Well, you've really grown!"

"You have too, Copper. I saw you coming back in the truck."

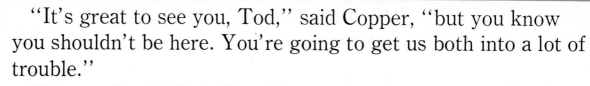

"It's great to see you, Tod," said Copper, "but you know you shouldn't be here. You're going to get us both into a lot of trouble."

"I know," said Tod, "but I just wanted to see you. That's all. We're still friends, aren't we, Copper?"

"Tod, those days are over. I'm—I'm a huntin' dog now. I'm trained to be a huntin' dog. You'd better get out of here before old Chief wakes up."

"That old dog doesn't worry me," said Tod.

"Listen, Tod, I'm serious," went on Copper. "Really

serious. You're—you're fair game as far as he is concerned. He'll think it is his duty to chase you. I can hear him waking up now."

Chief barked. Then he barked again, louder. The Hunter appeared at the cabin door, gun in hand as usual.

"It's that fox again," he shouted. "I'll get him this time."

He shot from the doorway, but missed, and Tod made off for the safety of the farmhouse.

The Widow heard the sound of barking and shooting and her light went on in the window. She opened the front door

and came out, holding a lantern. She was horrified to see Tod running for his life, being chased by two dogs.

"Oh, no! No!" she cried in anguish. "They're after Tod!"

The Hunter, Chief and Copper were in full cry, speeding down the hill.

"After him, boys. Go and get him!" shouted the Hunter.

Tod squeezed under the fence and jumped over a fallen log. A second afterwards a bullet bounced off the log, where he had jumped.

The dogs, working together as they had been taught, chased

after him. The gap gradually closed.

Tod looked quickly back over his shoulder and saw that Chief was not far behind. He was going uphill now, towards the railway, where he darted under a pile of spare rails stacked beside the track.

Chief lost the scent for a few seconds, but Copper picked it up and found Tod's hiding place. They both heard the Hunter's voice calling, "Copper! Copper! Copper!"

Copper looked down at Tod, breathless and trembling. "Tod—I don't want to see you get killed. I'll let you go free just this once. But I can't spare your life again. Do you understand?"

The Hunter was getting closer and closer, yelling, "Track 'im down, boy. Track 'im down."

He stopped by Tod's hiding place. "Which way did he go, Copper? Don't lose him now."

Copper gave his hunting howl and trotted away to the right, the Hunter following, and Tod emerged from under the rails. He knew the hunt was not over. He was not safe yet.

Tod trotted briskly along the railway track and was surprised and horrified when Chief sprang from behind a rock, and gave chase. The Hunter saw what was happening and yelled, "There they are! Good old Chief has got him on the run. We'll get that fox at last. Go to it, Chief!"

As Chief followed Tod, the yellow lights of a train showed round a bend, spearing the darkness.

Tod, scared to death but quick and nimble, dived under the train as it rumbled by.

"Jump, Chief, jump!" shouted the Hunter, "jump for your life!"

Chief jumped to avoid the train, but he was not quite in time. The front of the train struck him on the head, and he was hurled down a ravine beside the track. He rolled over and over, and landed in a shallow stream at the bottom.

Copper ran up and slithered down the slope to go to the help of his hunting partner.

The water was half over Chief's head, and at first Copper thought he was dead, and gave a dismal howl. Then he saw one of Chief's eyes open and close. He poked at Chief's body with his nose to try to get it nearer the bank, and he could feel the great dog breathing, which made him push harder. They had shared so many hunting trips in the camp on the mountain that they had become attached to each other.

Copper got Chief as much out of the water as he could, then he rested and looked up. There, at the top of the bank on the railway track, stood Tod, safe and sound.

"Tod," said Copper angrily, "Tod—if it's the last thing I ever do, I'll get you for this! I'll pay you out for what's happened to poor old Chief."

When Tod ran towards the glow of her lantern, the Widow fell on her knees and he ran straight into her arms. They hugged each other and Tod licked her face lovingly.

"Oh, Tod—thank heaven you're safe."

Outside the cabin, Copper sat sadly in front of his barrel, head drooping and an expression of misery on his face.

Soon the door of the cabin flew open, and the Hunter strode out with his gun. He slammed the door behind him and marched across the yard.

Copper shrunk back into his barrel. He knew his master had made up his mind to kill Tod at all costs, and get even with him for Chief's accident, which the fox had caused. Copper looked even more miserable. He blamed himself for letting Tod escape and not showing the Hunter where he was hiding.

"Oh, poor old Chief!" he thought, "it's all my fault that he's in trouble. I shouldn't have let Tod go free, I know I shouldn't."

Inside the farmhouse, in the kitchen, the Widow was sitting in her rocking chair, knitting. Tod was beside the hot stove, curled up in his basket. Although he was half asleep, he sensed that something was wrong. He raised his head and sniffed the air. He pricked his ears and listened intently. Then he sprang out of his basket and hid behind the stove.

The Widow looked up from her knitting. She heard nothing at all except the fire crackling and the clock ticking.

"Tod," she said, "whatever makes you so restless? There's nothing to be afraid of in this kitchen. Nothing at all."

Just then there was a heavy pounding on the door that made the whole room shake. The loud, rough voice of the Hunter sounded from outside.

"Widow, come out here," he shouted. "That fox of yours almost killed Chief and I'm going to get him."

"Stop behaving like a mad man, barging on to my private

property. You won't get into my farmhouse however hard you bang on the door, so there!" The Widow drew the two heavy bolts into position.

"You can't keep that fox of yours shut up for ever," bellowed the Hunter. "It isn't possible. I know he's somewhere in there."

Tod peeped round the stove but, seeing the furious Hunter through the window, he quickly dived back to his hiding place.

At last the Hunter gave up knocking and trying the door. The bolts held, however hard he pushed. He stamped off, muttering under his breath that he'd be back later, never fear.

The Widow and Tod settled down again, but both were uneasy. The farmhouse didn't feel as safe as usual.

Even Big Mama, Boomer and Dinky found it hard to sleep.

Tod's New Life

The next day the Widow was up and dressed early. When Tod woke and looked up from his basket, he saw she was putting on her hat in front of the glass. Her face looked sad and Tod ran towards her and felt relieved when she held out her arms and he jumped into them.

They left the farmhouse together, and Tod was pleased to see the Ford standing ready outside. He jumped into the front seat and the car started.

Tod loved going for a drive and looking out of the window. When they passed the Hunter's cabin he was carrying a load of wood across the yard. He stopped to watch the car go by, wondering where the Widow and her fox were off to, so early in the morning.

Tod was watching through the back window, and was glad to see the cabin fade into the distance.

The Widow began to sing softly, often glancing at Tod, who was listening to every word:

We met, it seems,
such a short time ago.
You looked at me—
needing me so.
Yet from your sadness
our happiness grew,
And so I found out
I needed you too.
I remember
how we used to play,

I recall
those rainy days:
The fire's glow
that kept us warm.
And now I find
we're both alone.
Goodbye may seem forever,
farewell is like the end,
But in my heart's memory
there you'll always be.

Tod did not know yet, but the Widow had made up her mind that she could not keep him safe any longer. However carefully she shut doors and windows, the Hunter might get in, or Tod slip out, and she knew that if those two met it would be the end of Tod. So she had decided to drive the little fox to a game reserve, and leave him there.

The game reserve was a large area of country where the wild animals were allowed to lead their natural lives. They could live, and breed, and bring up their young undisturbed by human beings. No one was allowed to enter the reserve with a gun or a trap.

As the Widow reached the game reserve and drove deeper in among the trees, she stopped singing and her face became sadder and sadder. Tod could not understand because he felt lively and cheerful. He liked the quiet feeling among the trees, with only the birds chirping.

The car stopped in a lovely, sunlit glade with soft grass and moss. They both got out, the Widow with tears in her eyes.

She took Tod up in her arms and carried him further from the track, down narrow, winding paths where no car could go.

Tod often licked her cheek, which was his way of trying to comfort her.

Then she set him down on the ground and undid his collar. Tod looked up with a puzzled expression. He knew he was supposed to wear his collar always. The Widow gave him one more hug and walked off, carrying his collar in her hand. Tod began to follow her.

"No, Tod, no," said the Widow. "Not this time. Stay where you are and you'll be safe."

The tears were now rolling down her cheeks as she shook a finger at Tod, which was a sign that she meant what she said. Tod knew he must obey and he forced himself to sit still while the Widow disappeared into the distance, going back to the car.

A few heavy drops of rain fell and the sky suddenly darkened. There were brilliant flashes of lightning and loud rolls of thunder. Tod dived for shelter among the bushes.

As the Widow drove her car past the cabin, towards the farmhouse, the Hunter was watching for her. He loosened Copper's lead and crouched with him beside his barrel.

"I know what she's up to," said the Hunter. "She's dropped that fox off in the game reserve. She thinks he's safe there, but we'll get him—we'll get him."

Meanwhile, the injured Chief was recovering in the cabin, lying on a soft rug. "This suits me," he said to himself. "Good food. Warm stove. Soft blanket. It's a lot better than sleeping in that cold barrel outside."

The Hunter went into the cabin and called Copper's name, "Copper! Copper! Come here, will you."

Copper ran indoors, tail wagging, but hesitated when he saw what the Hunter was doing. He was standing with a wicked-looking steel trap in his hand. It was open, showing its cruel, iron teeth. Copper was frightened, he hardly knew why.

"If that sneaky fox comes sniffing round here, we'll be ready for him," said the Hunter. He shut the trap with a loud click, and the iron teeth came together.

"We'll make an end of that red devil."

Away in the game reserve, Tod was terrified of the lightning. He looked round for a safe place where he could hide. He saw the mouth of a burrow and crept thankfully inside, but the burrow was the home of an old badger who was angry at being disturbed.

"Out! Out! Where do you think you're going?" he shouted.

Tod tried to explain: "Excuse me, please, I was just—trying to—"

"Barge into someone's house as if you owned it," put in the

badger. "Tarryhooting around the woods—waking up folks in the middle of the night."

"I honestly didn't know anybody lived here," said Tod meekly.

"Well, you know now. Get off my property—go on, beat it!"

Tod hastily retreated backwards and felt something prickling him. He had run into a porcupine.

"I've been watching you, sir. You can stay with me if you like. You're welcome," said the porcupine, politely.

Tod hesitated just a moment as he looked at the porcupine's sharp quills, but he longed for a safe, dry bed for the night.

"That's very nice of you," he said, and the two of them arranged themselves contentedly inside the hollow tree which was the porcupine's home. Tod was careful not to lie too close to his prickly companion.

The next morning, Big Mama flew over the nature reserve, looking for Tod. As she rested on a branch, she thought she saw him under some bushes. It was an animal just about his colour and shape.

"Tod! Tod!" she cried.

The animal came from under the bush. It was *not* Tod, but a young vixen, which is a female fox.

"Hello, Big Mama," said the vixen, whose name was Vixey. "What brings you this way?"

"I'm looking for a fox named Tod. He's new to this forest."

"New is he?" said Vixey, showing interest. "Tell me what this Tod looks like."

"Oh," said Big Mama. "He's young—about your age—and handsome."

"He sounds very attractive," said Vixey. "I'm not doing anything special just now, I'll help you find him."

"Come along then, honey. He must be somewhere."

While Big Mama and Vixey began their search, the porcupine woke up, yawning, and stretched. He rolled against Tod, who woke to find a dozen sharp quills pricking his skin. He let out a great yell of alarm and fell out of the hole in the tree, landing, most unluckily, on top of the cross badger, who had just come out of his burrow to have a breath of air.

"Wow!" screamed Tod. "What's happened? Wherever am I? Help!"

"You're on top of me," growled the badger. "You barged in on me last night and here you are again!"

"Mr. Digger, sir, it *was* an accident. I saw it."

"You keep out of this, you walking pincushion!"

"You shouldn't be so grumpy to someone who's new to the neighbourhood," went on the porcupine.

"A stranger, eh? Why don't you go back where you came from? Well, get going—be off!"

Tod, feeling unhappy and unwanted, walked slowly away. He'd like nothing better than to go back where he came from, to the farmhouse and the Widow and his warm basket by the fire. But it wasn't possible.

Big Mama and Vixey saw Tod walking miserably away, head down and tail drooping.

Vixey felt sorry for him.

"He seems so unhappy, Big Mama."

"Well, you can't blame him," said Big Mama. "He was dropped out here and left all alone, without a friend in the world."

"Perhaps there's something I could do to cheer him up?" suggested Vixey.

"Honey, those are magic words. I think there's a lot you could do. Now you stand still just where you are. Leave it to me."

Big Mama flew after Tod and landed just in front of him. He looked even worse close to, with dirt on his fur and dead leaves sticking to him.

"Good morning, Tod."

"Oh, hello, Big Mama."

"Last night was pretty miserable for you, wasn't it, honey?"

"Just terrible."

"Well, cheer up, Tod. Look around you. The forest is looking beautiful this morning. Really beautiful."

"After last night *nothing* looks beautiful to me. Nothing at all," Tod said in despair.

A New Friend

Tod did what Big Mama had suggested and turned his head. He soon saw Vixey, standing in a shaft of sunshine, which brought out the red-brown of her glossy coat and made her white parts gleam like snow. Her shape was delicate and attractive.

"Who is that?" he gasped.

"Oh, just another fox, a *lady* fox," explained Big Mama.

"Isn't she beautiful! I wonder what her name is?"

"Why don't you go and ask her?"

"I think I will," said Tod and went over to Vixey.

"Hello!" he said. "May I call you by your first name?"

"Oh, yes," said Vixey. "It's Vixey."

"My name is Tod."

"That's a very nice name," said Vixey.

They walked together to the edge of the stream, which was sparkling in the sunlight. Tod could not take his eyes off his new companion.

"This stream is just full of trout," said Vixey. "Do you think you could catch one for me?"

"Of course I can," said Tod eagerly, though he had never caught a trout in his life. He wanted to impress Vixey and show her how clever he was.

"Now watch me—I'm an expert at fishing."

There was a log floating in the stream and Tod walked out on it.

"Oh Tod, don't show off!" warned Big Mama.

"I know all the tricks," boasted Tod. "Here comes a whopper! Watch me very closely."

He balanced on the very end of the log and put in a paw to scoop up the fish. But he missed and showered Vixey with water, as he fell off the tilting log with a mighty splash. Tod floundered about and snapped at something he imagined was the fish, but he was mistaken. It was only a stick. He scrambled on to the bank calling out, "I've got him!"

He looked so funny with the stick in his mouth that Big Mama and Vixey burst out laughing. So did Boomer and Dinky who were watching from a branch.

"Oh Tod," laughed Vixey, "you're the funniest thing I ever saw."

Tod was terribly upset when he saw her laughing. She was

the one person in the world he wanted to impress.

"Go on, laugh at me like everyone else round here," he said in a hurt voice.

"I'm sorry, Tod," said Vixey. "But I really couldn't help it. You were so funny."

"You're just an empty-headed female," said Tod.

"You've got a nerve. Why don't you grow up?" replied Vixey.

Tod and Vixey sat with their backs to each other, angry and unhappy. They wanted to be friends, but there they were in the middle of a dreadful quarrel.

Big Mama sang some good advice to Tod:

*When you have
a natural attraction,
You deserve
a mutual reaction.
You're going to get
a lot of satisfaction
When you feel that
natural affection
Leads you in the
positive direction.*

Tod walked away from Vixey and found himself in a patch of bright, forest flowers. He picked one in his teeth and turned round and offered it to Vixey, who smelt it and accepted it. She licked Tod's cheek and cuddled up to him. They nuzzled each other lovingly.

Big Mama tried to shoo the other animals away—Boomer and Dinky and the badger and the porcupine—so that Tod and Vixey could get to know each other in peace.

"I know you're going to love the forest, Tod," said Vixey. "Let me show you around. I'll take you everywhere and show you everything."

She led the way and Tod followed.

Early the next morning, the Hunter and Copper approached the game reserve. They reached the sign saying NO HUNTING in big, black letters.

"No hunting?" the Hunter read. "Well, now, we aren't
exactly going huntin'. We're just going to get a no-good fox.
That's what we're going to do."

He got out a pair of strong wire-cutters and snipped through
the strands of wire making the fence. They curled back.

The Hunter and his hound were now inside the game
reserve. The Hunter sent Copper off to try to pick up the
fox's scent.

NO HUNTING
GAME PRESERVE

"All right, boy. Get tracking."

Copper ran on ahead, sniffing the air and the ground, and getting deeper and deeper into the forest. A squirrel watched from a branch and a porcupine stuck his head out of a hole. The Hunter followed silently behind, carrying his gun and his steel traps.

Copper came to a stream, stopped, and began sniffing along the bank. He growled softly.

"What have you found there, Copper?" The Hunter bent down and saw a fox's tracks clearly printed in the muddy ground. "Good work, boy. He'll be coming right through here, heading for the water—but he won't be drinking any."

A little way off, Tod and Vixey came out of the burrow where they had spent the night together.

"What a great day to be alive, Vixey," said Tod. "I've never been happier than I am now."

"Oh Tod, me too, me too."

They nuzzled each other and went off into the wood. As

they went, the Hunter, out of sight, was quickly setting his traps down by the water. He filled his hat with leaves and sprinkled them over the traps to hide them. No one could guess that strong, cruel teeth lay below, ready to clash together.

The two foxes reached the edge of the forest and Vixey paused.

"What is it, Vixey?
What's wrong?"

"I don't want to go any further, Tod. It's too quiet."

Tod went on slowly and Vixey cried out, "Tod—do be careful."

Tod sensed danger and smelt it, too. He passed so near one of the traps that his hind leg actually disturbed some of the leaves piled on top.

The Hunter's gun gave a slight click. Tod jumped into the air and the trap went off, *just* missing his paw. He turned and ran down the path that led back to Vixey.

The Hunter began shooting and, as Tod leapt over a log, bits of wood flew up all round him.

Copper joined his master and heard him say, "Blast that fox! I've missed him again."

Tod joined Vixey and told her to head straight for the burrow. Copper was hard on Tod's heels as he, too, dived into

the burrow after Vixey. Copper began to dig furiously to try to get the foxes out. The Hunter appeared and started to fire wildly into the burrow, mad with rage that Tod seemed to have escaped. Tod and Vixey cowered together deep in the darkest part.

Copper was digging so strongly that he had nearly made the entrance big enough to get through himself. He was clawing at the earth, when Tod saw what was happening and bit him on the paw. Copper yelped with pain, and then started to dig again with even more energy.

When the Hunter saw that his hound had been injured, he began to tear up handfuls of grass and weeds, and stack them by the front and back entrances to the burrow. He prepared to set them on fire, while he and Copper waited by each entrance ready to catch the foxes when they were forced out into the open.

The weeds smoked and smouldered, and then burst into flames. Vixey began to cough and choke with the clouds of smoke.

"We're trapped, Tod," she gasped. "We're trapped."

Tod thought quickly. They must do something soon before the fire got worse.

"This is our only chance, Vixey. Now—run for it!"

The two terrified foxes burst through the smoke and flames and made off. The Hunter could not believe his eyes.

"Oh, no! I don't believe it, I simply don't believe it."

Copper growled and sped away after the fleeing foxes, but the smoke made it difficult to follow their trail as they turned and twisted among rocks and bushes, running together.

Tod and Vixey, knowing they were still in danger, made their way up a high cliff. Copper picked up their scent again and followed close behind, weaving his way over rock and under bush, nose well down.

Friends for Ever

Tod was thinking of a scheme to out-wit Copper. He made a sign to Vixey which meant: "Follow me". He jumped up on to a tree and leapt from the tree to a log, which was bridging a waterfall. He looked back over his shoulder and saw Vixey gathering all her strength to leap on to the log. She managed to land safely.

Copper lost the trail at the base of the tree and sniffed around. The Hunter joined him and they stood among the roots of the tree, both looking puzzled. Whatever could have happened?

The Hunter's gun was fully loaded and he was ready to fire instantly when the moment came. The sun was in their eyes and they were both taken completely by surprise when an enormous grizzly bear reared up above them. Though the Hunter was shaking with fear, his trembling hands managed to squeeze the trigger, but the shot only grazed the shoulder of the grizzly.

The bear was now enraged with pain and moved towards the Hunter, forcing him backwards, nearer to the edge of the cliff. He frantically pulled a bullet out of his pocket and inserted it into the gun, only to have the gun swept from his hands by a mighty swipe from a gigantic paw.

The Hunter lost his balance and tumbled down the cliff. At the bottom he staggered to his feet, and stepped backwards, straight into one of his own steel traps. The trap closed with a snap, as it had closed on many defenceless furry animals in

the past. The Hunter was held fast in its cruel jaws.

He sat down to try to loosen the trap and free his foot, but the sight of the grizzly advancing towards him made him shaky and clumsy. He was held fast and was utterly at the bear's mercy.

But there was help at hand. Copper dashed in to try to save his master's life. He leapt at the bear's neck and tried to bite it, as he had been trained, but the bear threw him to the ground. He at once tried a second time, and got a stronger grip on the bear's neck, and though the bear shook himself violently, the dog held on grimly.

Then the grizzly threw himself on to the ground, trying to hit Copper's head.

Copper howled with pain and the sound reached Tod, who hesitated a moment. Should he stay and protect Vixey, his mate, or go and help an old friend? He soon made up his mind. Just as the bear was lifting a huge paw ready to strike—and kill—Copper, a red blur hurled itself through the air, snarling and scratching, and fastened sharp teeth in the bear's ear.

Copper lifted his head and realised that his friend, Tod, had come to help him.

The bear shook his great head to try to shake off the fox, but Tod clung on. At last the bear prised him loose and flung him up in the air, and he landed on the log that spanned the waterfall. He lay there stunned. The bear lumbered after him but his great weight was too much for the half-rotten log.

With a loud crack, the log broke in two and fell with the bear and the fox into the wild, white water below.

The grizzly was swept away downstream, but Tod was lucky. The foaming water tossed him on to a sand-bank. He was lying there, dazed and exhausted, when he felt a familiar, warm nose push against his. He looked up and saw Copper standing beside him, smiling. They were together once more.

But Tod was not yet out of danger. The Hunter had freed his foot from the trap and was limping towards them, gun raised to his shoulder.

"Get out of the way, Copper."

Copper simply covered Tod's body with his own, so the Hunter could not shoot the fox without shooting the dog.

"Get out of the way, Copper!"

Still Copper never moved an inch, looking up into his master's face, begging him to understand.

The Hunter slowly lowered his gun and patted Copper's head lovingly. "Let's go home," he said gently, limping off. Copper followed at his heels, looking back many times to exchange farewell glances with Tod.

A few days later, things were normal once more at the Hunter's cabin and the Widow's farm. Dinky and Boomer were busy on a tree near the farm, still hunting for Squeeks the caterpillar. They were surprised when a lovely butterfly fluttered out into the sunshine, escaping from the barn through a knot-hole in the wood.

It landed on the woodpecker's beak. The woodpecker stuttered, "Dinky! Look! There's something very familiar about this creature's eyes. . . ."

"No—it couldn't be, could it?" said Dinky.

The butterfly took off, and Big Mama waved goodbye as it disappeared among the trees.

Boomer and Dinky had learned something new: that caterpillars turn into butterflies.

Down by the cabin, Chief and Copper watched with amusement while the Widow, trying her best to be neighbourly, attended to the Hunter's wounded leg on the porch. The two old enemies had become friends.

"Will you keep still there while I bandage you up. You're behaving like a child!"

"Oh, do be careful! Ooh!—Ow!—"

"He really is making a fuss over a little hurt leg," said Chief.

Copper grinned and, closing his eyes, he thought over all that had happened.

"Tod," thought Copper, remembering, "you're my very best friend."

"And you're mine too, Copper. And we'll always be friends. For ever . . ."

While Copper remembered old times, he lifted his head and gazed up at the distant cliff. There, against the skyline, were Tod and Vixey looking down.